This book belongs to:

....

This book is dedicated to Maisha, Madiha and Ubayd.

ISBN-13: 978-1539583066

www.mhcreativity.co.uk
twitter account:@MoyHoq

George

The World's Most Flexible Bird

Author & Illustrator

Moynul Hoque

www.mhcreativity.co.uk

This is George and he is a special bird. He has the gift to stretch his body like a rubber band.

Now, let's see what type of objects George can wrap and twist around.

George is so

flexible

he can wrap around a lamp post.

George is so

springy

he can twist around a submarine.

George is so

bendy

he can wrap around a hot air balloon.

George is so

stretchy

he can twist around an enormous elephant.

George is so

elastic

he can wrap around an aeroplane.

George is so

bendable

he can twist around a school bus.

SCHOOL BUS
SCHOOL BUS

George is so

rubber-like

he can wrap around a space rocket.

George is so

moldable

he can twist around a lighthouse.

George is so

spaghetti-like

he can wrap around the moon.

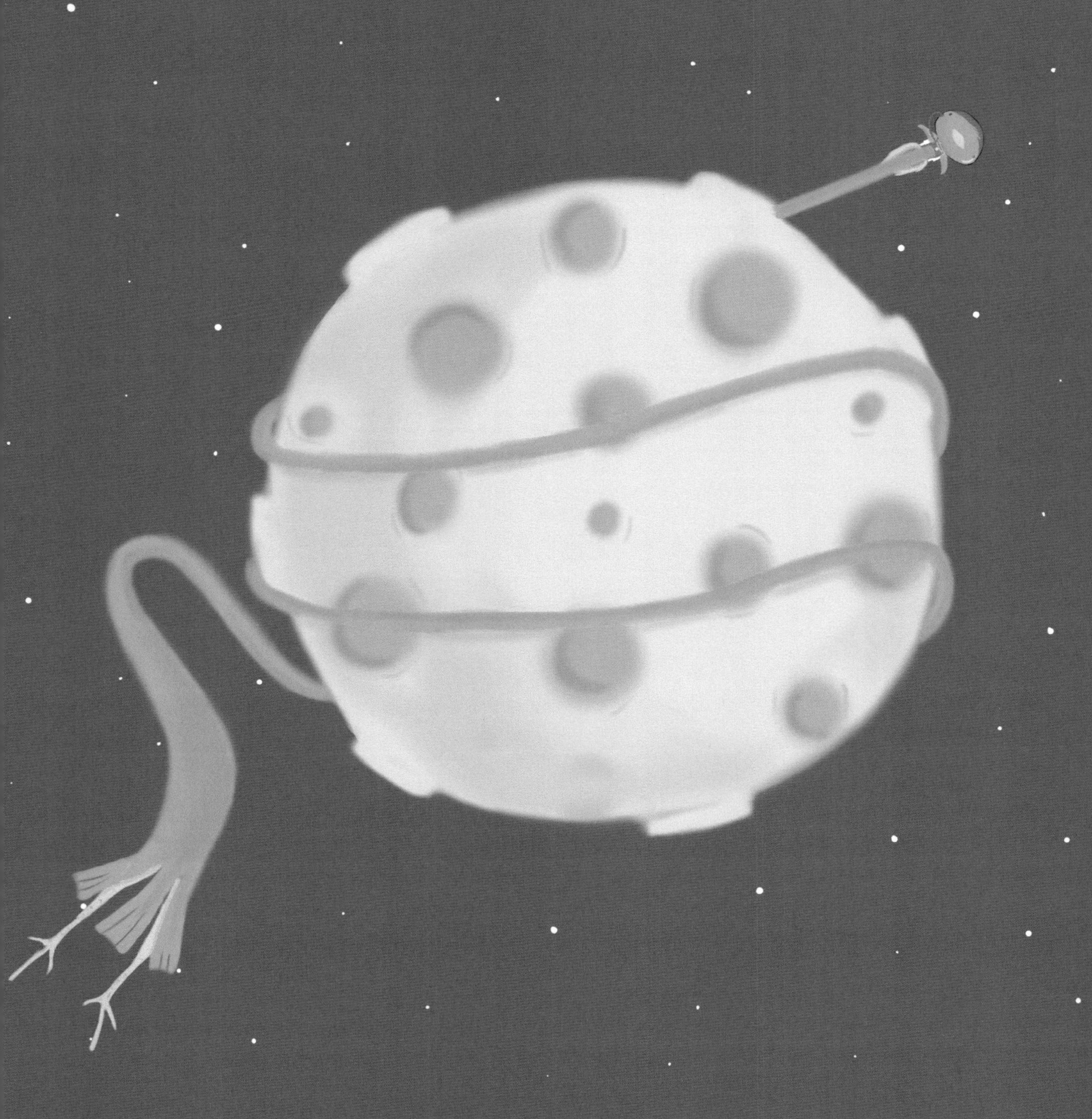

But most of all, George enjoys being a normal bird.

And he likes to fly with his friends, eat fat juicy worms, and sing on top of roof-tops.

The End

to visit my website and discover my latest book releases.

www.mhcreativity.co.uk

8426329R00018

Printed in Germany
by Amazon Distribution
GmbH, Leipzig